Five Favourite Tales

Five
Favourite Tales

Five Favourite Tales

Contents

The Costume Ball

It was the day of the Costume Ball and Angelina hadn't been invited. "If you're going as a queen and Dad's going as a king, it makes sense that I go as a princess!" she said to Mrs Mouseling.

"I'm sorry Angelina," said Mrs Mouseling patiently. "The ball is for grown ups, not little mouselings!"

"Everyone should be allowed to go to the ball," complained Angelina to Alice later. Her friend emerged from the dressing up box wearing a hat and a dress that was far too big for her.

Alice danced until she tripped over the hem and fell on top of Angelina. "Sorry!" she giggled. "You could fit us both in this dress!"
"Yes . . ." said Angelina thoughtfully.

It was almost time for the Costume Ball
to begin and Mrs Mouseling looked
beautiful.
"Mrs Hodgepodge will be here to
babysit any minute," she said.
"Oh, no!" groaned Angelina. "Last time
she kept me awake all night with her
horrible snoring!"
"I hope she doesn't bring her cabbage
jelly," whispered Alice.

Mr Mouseling came into the room
dressed like a giant bee instead of a king.
"Mix up at the costume shop!" he
explained, as Angelina and Alice giggled.

Just then Mrs Hodgepodge arrived.
"Good night you two," said Mrs
Mouseling as she swept out of the door
on Mr Mouseling's arm.
"Be good for Mrs Hodgepodge!"

After a horrible dinner of cabbage jelly,
Angelina and Alice ran upstairs.
"I wish we were at the ball," sighed
Angelina. "Would you care to dance?"
"I'd love to," smiled Alice.

Downstairs Mrs Hodgepodge had
fallen asleep and was beginning to snore
loudly. Angelina was trying to listen to
the beautiful music drifting through the
window from the Ball.

"Right. Come on Alice!" exclaimed
Angelina, as she began rummaging
through the dressing-up box.
"Come on where?" asked Alice.
"To the Costume Ball of course!"

"But what about Mrs Hodgepodge?"
whispered Alice.
"She'll be asleep for hours!" replied
Angelina, tossing a hat over to Alice.

As Angelina and Alice entered the hall,
they gasped.
"Wow! Look Alice! It's wonderful!"
smiled Angelina. From within their
disguise, the two mouselings looked
around them. Angelina wobbled on
Alice's shoulders as they tottered
towards a table piled with delicious
things to eat.
"All that fooood!" cried Alice.

"Careful Alice!" whispered Angelina as
Alice grabbed a cheese ball.
"Such a wonderful party, don't you
agree, my dear?" asked a familiar voice.

It was Miss Lilly!
"Err yes, Miss . . . miss . . . absolutely unmissable!" stuttered Angelina in her most grown-up voice.

Luckily, just then Dr Tuttle appeared.
"I was wondering if you'd care to
dance?" he asked Miss Lilly.
"It would be a pleasure, darlink!" she
replied as she took his paw.
"See you later for the Whiskers Reel!"
said Miss Lilly as she disappeared.
"I wish someone would ask me to
dance," said Angelina glumly as she
watched them make their way onto the
crowded dance floor.

Back at the Mouseling's cottage, Mrs Hodgepodge woke up when she felt a draft. "It's coming from Angelina's room," she muttered as she went to investigate. The window was wide open.

At the ball, Angelina was desperate to dance when a voice announced, "Take your positions for the Whiskers Reel!" "Come on Alice!" she whispered. Everyone lined up and the music started.

As they danced, Angelina began to lose her balance on Alice's shoulders. She wobbled, and bumped into her father, but luckily he didn't recognize her. Then they stumbled into the table, and cheese balls flew everywhere as the two mouselings landed in a sticky heap.

Just at that moment, Mrs Hodgepodge threw open the doors of the hall.

"There they are, those naughty little runaways!" she cried.
"Angelina!" gasped Mr and Mrs Mouseling.

Everyone stared at the two mouselings as they sat on the floor, surrounded by cheese balls and trying hard not to cry.

Now they were in real trouble.

Angelina and Alice were up early the
next morning. There was a great deal
of mess to be cleared up in the hall.

"My back's aching! This is such hard
work!" groaned Alice, mopping the floor.
"I'm so tired! Perhaps going to the
ball wasn't such a good idea," sighed
Angelina as she scrubbed away.

The door opened and Mrs Mouseling
came in with Mrs Hodgepodge.
"We've brought you something to eat!"
said Angelina's mother, smiling.

Angelina and Alice took huge bites from
the delicious looking sandwiches.

"Oh, no!" they groaned.
"Cabbage jelly!"

Angelina in the Wings

"I have wonderful news!" said Miss Lilly one day after class. "As you know, the famous Madame Zizi is to perform 'The Sun Queen' at the theatre!"

"And she is coming here tomorrow with
Mr Popoff, the director, to take a class
with you!"
Everyone gasped with delight.
"One of the little sunbeams in the ballet
has mousepox," Miss Lilly continued.
"Does that mean they need another
sunbeam?" asked Angelina, hardly
daring to believe it.
"It does Angelina! Indeed it does!"
smiled Miss Lilly.

That evening at supper, Cousin Henry
was running round the kitchen,
playing with his clockwork ladybird
and singing. He was very excited
about Angelina being a sunbeam.

Angelina, however, was getting nervous.
"Don't worry," said Mrs Mouseling.
"You'll have Henry as your mascot!"
"WHAT!" Angelina was horrified.
"I have to take Henry to the audition?"

"I'll be the best mascot ever!" said Henry,
spilling his drink. "What's a mascot?"
"Someone who brings luck," said Mrs
Mouseling cheerfully.
Angelina groaned.

The next day at class, Angelina felt very
nervous as she got ready. Mr Popoff was
going to take the lesson so that Madame
Zizi could watch the mouselings dance.
Henry sat at the side of the room,
playing with his ladybird and trying
to keep still.

"Alice!" whispered Angelina to her best
friend as they began to dance. "This
sunbeam is about to shine!"

As Angelina spun round the room,
she hissed at Henry to sit quietly.
"Zee leetle peenk mouseling," said
Madame Zizi suddenly.
"On your own please!" said Mr Popoff.

"Enchantée!" exclaimed Madame Zizi, as she watched Angelina dance on her own.

Suddenly a fly landed on Henry's nose, making him drop his ladybird!
"Oh, no!" he cried, chasing it across the floor. The ladybird bumped into Angelina, and over she toppled.
"What a sweet mouseling!" said Madame Zizi, spotting Henry. "He must be our sunbeam! Zee peenk one can understudy."

"I can't believe Henry got the part!" sobbed Angelina that evening. "And I just have to stand and watch! It's so unfair!" Alice tried to comfort her.

"But when Madame Zizi sees how good you are, she's bound to make room for another sunbeam!" she said cheerily, offering Angelina a cheesy niblet.

The next day, all the sunbeams, and
Angelina, danced in perfect time.
Apart from Henry.
"Jump like Angelina!" said Mr Popoff.

Henry tried hard but it was very difficult
for such a tiny mouse.
"Move back, Angelina!" continued Mr
Popoff. "They must do it alone!"

That evening, Angelina rang Alice. "How can I get Madame Zizi to notice me?" she cried desperately.

Henry was dancing around the room and Mrs Mouseling came in just as he tripped over Angelina's ballet things, thrown carelessly on the floor. "Oh, Angelina! I'm not your servant!" she scolded, picking everything up. Servant! thought Angelina. That's a good idea!

The next day, Angelina did everything for Madame Zizi. She ran around fetching and carrying until she was exhausted. Just before the rehearsal, she even helped with her costume!

"Where is the little boy mouseling?"
asked Mr Popoff impatiently a few
minutes later. "We are ready to start!"
Everyone looked around.
"Here I am!" sang Henry, running onto
the stage a little out of breath.
He'd got a bit lost backstage.

Madame Zizi swept him into her arms.
"Eet is not his fault," she said. "Angelina
should have been looking after him like
I told her too!"

Later, Alice tried to cheer up Angelina.
"Only one more day to go then I'm a
sunbeam!" smiled Henry happily.
Angelina began to sob.

Then, Angelina and Alice heard Mr
Popoff's voice coming from the stage.
"Zizi, we have to bring on the understudy
Sunbeam! The boy mouseling must go!"
Angelina was stunned.

"Please give him another chance," Angelina
cried. "I can help him. I promise!"
Madame Zizi agreed. "Yes, Popoff! You
weel geev him one more chance at the
dress rehearsal tomorrow. I inseest!"

That evening Angelina watched as
Henry struggled with the difficult steps.
"Well done!" she said. "Now we'll try it
again. Watch me!"

At last it was time for the dress rehearsal.
At the theatre, the sunbeams waited in
their dressing room with Mr Popoff,
ready to go on stage.

Suddenly, Madame Zizi rushed in.
"Whatever is the matter, Zizi?" asked
Mr Popoff nervously.
"Disaster!" she replied. "Another one of
our leetle sunbeams has the mousepox!"

Angelina had her chance at last! The little
sunbeams danced their hearts out, and at
the end of the performance took their bows
behind the famous Madame Zizi.

As the performers left the stage, the
applause was deafening. Mr and Mrs
Mouseling, Henry's parents, Alice
and Miss Lilly leapt to their feet and
clapped as hard as they could. They all
felt so proud.
"Oh, Henry! You were wonderful,"
said Angelina breathlessly.
"You were indeed perfect, Henry,"
smiled Mr Popoff. "And it was all down
to you, Angelina!"

The next morning, Angelina and Henry
sat side by side in bed, covered in pink
mousepox spots!
Suddenly, they heard a knock on the
bedroom door.

"Room service," laughed Mrs Mouseling,
popping her head round the door.
"I've brought you some cheesy niblets,
sent by Alice, for two spectacular
spotty sunbeams!"

Angelina's
Dance of Friendship

"Well done, my darlings!" said Miss Lilly at the end of ballet class. "Now, before you go, I have some news."

The mouselings gathered around. "Do you remember Anya Moussorsky, who visited from Dacovia last year?" asked Miss Lilly. "Anya is coming here this summer to learn ballet."

"Oh, Alice!" Angelina squealed. "Isn't that wonderful?"

That evening, Angelina pleaded with her
mother to let Anya stay at their house.
"Please, Mum," said Angelina. "She won't
be any trouble!"
"But where will she sleep?" said Mrs
Mouseling.
"In my room," Angelina insisted. She
went over to her father and tugged his
arm gently. "I *want* to share my room!"

Angelina's room was a bit crowded with
two beds, but Angelina was too excited
to care. "We're going to have the best
summer ever," she said when Anya
finally arrived. "We'll share everything!"

Angelina cleared some space on the nightstand for Anya's books and her picture of her parents. And she pulled a pink tutu out of her closet for Anya to wear to ballet class.

"Thanks, Angelina," said Anya, "but I've never done ballet before. What if I don't fit in?"

Angelina put an arm around her friend. "Don't worry, Anya," she said. "I'll look after you. I promise."

At ballet class the next day, Anya worked
very hard to follow Angelina's steps.
"You dance so well, Anya!" exclaimed
Alice when the music ended. "It's as if
you've been doing ballet for ages."

When Miss Lilly asked the mouselings
to choose partners to make up a special
dance, Angelina was worried. Would Alice
be hurt if Angelina danced with Anya?
But Alice didn't mind at all, and Anya had
a wonderful idea – she knew a perfect
story for her and Angelina to dance.

"It's a Dacovian story," explained Anya,
"about two kingfishers who are friends
and stay together their whole lives."

"How lovely!" said Miss Lilly. "A dance
of friendship." She pulled the two
mouselings into a warm embrace.

Angelina and Anya practised their
special dance every day at ballet class.
Anya's steps soon became as graceful
as Angelina's.

"Anya, you are doing so well!" Miss Lilly
said when they had finished their dance.

Then Miss Lilly pulled Angelina aside.
"The Dacovian Ballet is coming to the
Theatre Royale again," said Miss Lilly.
"I think it's a good idea for me to invite
Anya this year, don't you?"

Angelina was terribly disappointed.
Miss Lilly always took her to the
Dacovian Ballet. It wasn't fair!
But all Angelina could say was,
"Yes, Miss Lilly."

"Good, then," said Miss Lilly, patting
Angelina's shoulder. "And tell your
mother I'm looking forward to
dinner tonight."

That evening, everyone fussed over the Dacovian dinner that Anya had helped to prepare.

"I'm going to show Mrs Mouseling how to make cheese soufflé, too," Anya said to Miss Lilly, who sat across the table from her.

Angelina sighed and played with her food. She wished there was something else to talk about. Then she spotted the kingfisher costumes hanging in the corner. "What do you think of these, Miss Lilly?" Angelina asked brightly.

"They're beautiful!" said Miss Lilly.
"Anya is learning ballet so fast," she said
to Mrs Mouseling. "Soon she'll apply to
the Dacovian Ballet Academy!"

Anya, Anya, Anya, thought Angelina
miserably. *Why wouldn't everyone stop
talking about Anya?*

After dinner, Angelina found Anya sitting in the dark bedroom, staring at the picture of her parents. She looked lonely, and for a moment, Angelina felt sorry for her. Then Angelina realized where Anya was sitting.

"That's my bed!" Angelina snapped.

Anya jumped off the bed in surprise. "Oh!" she said. "But I thought we were sharing everything."

'I'm not so sure now," said Angelina. Jealous, angry words tumbled out of her mouth. "I'm tired of hearing about how talented you are," Angelina cried. 'And how great Dacovia is. Maybe you just should have stayed there!"

When Angelina awoke the next morning, she was feeling very sorry for the way she had acted. But when she turned to apologize to Anya, Angelina saw that Anya's bed was empty.

Angelina raced downstairs to the kitchen.
"Have you seen Anya?" Angelina asked
her mother desperately.
"No," said Mrs Mouseling. "Isn't she in
your room?"

Angelina rushed out the front door
without answering, but the sound of
the ringing telephone called her back.
"Oh, hello, Miss Lilly," said Mrs
Mouseling into the receiver. "Anya's
at your house? Good gracious! I had
no idea!"

Minutes later, Angelina sat, her head hung low, in Miss Lilly's parlour. She was too ashamed to look at Miss Lilly.

"I'm very disappointed in you," said Miss Lilly. "How would you like to be away from your parents for such a long time?"

"I wouldn't," Angelina answered in a small voice. "Oh, I've been so mean! Please, may I see Anya and apologize?"

"Of course you may," said Miss Lilly. She disappeared down the hall, and Angelina waited nervously in the parlour.

But when Miss Lilly returned, Anya wasn't with her. "Anya doesn't wish to see you," said Miss Lilly gently. "Perhaps you can speak to her at ballet class."

Angelina's heart sank. Would Anya ever forgive her?

At ballet class, Angelina spotted Anya across the room, talking with William. Angelina took a deep breath, then hurried over.

But Anya wasn't happy to see Angelina. "I don't want to dance with you," Anya said frostily. "I'm dancing with Alice."

After class, a very sad Angelina trudged home beside Alice. "I just wish she'd let me apologize," said Angelina.

Alice felt terrible. "I wish I could help," she said. "Anya wants to practise down by the river with me, wearing your costume so that we'll feel like real kingfishers."

Angelina stopped in her tracks and smiled thoughtfully. Now she knew just how to apologize to Anya.

Angelina dressed in her kingfisher
costume and hurried down to the river.
Anya was already there. "Hi, Alice!"
Anya called.

Angelina breathed a sigh of relief. Anya
didn't recognize her!

On the count of three, the mouselings began to dance. They fluttered apart and then swooped back together, just like real kingfishers. They dipped low and rose up again, wings outstretched.

When the dance ended, Angelina pulled off her mask. "I'm sorry, Anya," she whispered, hoping Anya wouldn't be angry that she had been fooled.

Anya was silent for a moment, and then she burst into tears. "I'm sorry, too!" she cried. She threw her arms open wide, and the two friends hugged each other.

Weeks later, after leaving the Theatre Royale, Angelina and Anya sat together in a bus seat, chattering excitedly. "Wasn't the prince amazing?" asked Angelina.

"Oh, yes," said Anya. "Thank you, Miss Lilly. It was the best show I've ever seen!"

Miss Lilly, who was seated behind the two mouselings, leaned forward. "And to think," she said, "that Angelina believed she wasn't going to the Dacovian Ballet this year, when I had three tickets all along!"

That evening, Anya started packing her things. She was going home tomorrow. She handed the pink tutu to Angelina.

"Oh, no," Angelina insisted. "Keep it. What's mine is yours, remember?" she said warmly, and *this* time, Angelina truly meant it.

A Day
at the Fair

"Excellent darlinks!" said Miss Lilly at the end of the dance class.

Angelina and her friend, Alice, rushed to get changed.

"Just think, Alice," said Angelina. "In exactly one hour, you and I will be riding on the fastest, scariest rollercoaster in all of Mouseland! Hurry up, William! We'll be late for the fair!"

Angelina rushed home and counted the money in her piggy bank. "Hooray!" she said, "just enough for a candy floss!" Scooping up the coins, she ran to the door.

Unfortunately she bumped straight into Mrs Mouseling and her cousin Henry.

"Excuse me young lady," said her mother. "You promised to look after Henry today." "But I'm going to the fair!" cried Angelina.

"Great!" said Henry. "I love fairs!"

Angelina sighed and, fixing a grin on
her face, took him by the hand.

When Angelina and Henry arrived at the
fair, they headed straight for the rides.
"Look at the merry-go-round, Angelina!
I love them. Don't you?" asked Henry.

"No Henry," said Angelina sniffily. "Merry-go-rounds are for babies."

"And there's a man selling balloons!" continued Henry. "Can I have a blue one? Please!"

"No you can't, Henry! I've only got enough money for a candy floss." They walked across the noisy fairground until Angelina found Alice and William.

The four mouselings rushed around the
noisy colourful fairground, looking at
all the different rides, until at last they
came to the big wheel. Henry could
hardly see the top of it. It seemed like a
very very long way up. Angelina was so
excited! She couldn't wait to jump on!

"I told you that I don't really like
big wheels," whispered Henry as he
squeezed Angelina's hand very tightly.

Angelina bent down to reassure him. "Don't worry, Henry they're not at all scary!" she said gently. "Trust me. You're going to love it!"

Henry reluctantly followed the others and up they went, climbing higher and higher.

"Isn't this fun, Henry?" laughed Angelina.

But poor Henry wasn't having fun at all. In fact he felt quite sick. "I want to get off!" he sobbed loudly.

Angelina was very embarrassed as the huge wheel came to a standstill and an attendant helped Henry step off the ride.

Henry held William's hand as the four
friends queued up for the Haunted House.
But Henry still wasn't happy.

"I told you Angelina! I hate the dark!"

Angelina ignored poor Henry and dragged
him inside. There were spooky noises
and it was almost pitch black! Suddenly,
Henry realized that he was no longer
holding William's hand. He was all alone!

Henry walked bravely through the darkness, until he thought he saw William. He reached out his hand. But, oh no! It was a huge hairy spider.

"Agghhhhh!" screamed Henry.

The lights went on and Henry looked
around him. It didn't look so scary
any more. He was very pleased to see
Angelina and the others just up ahead.

"I'm scared of spiders," sobbed Henry.
He felt very shy as the attendant led
them all out of the Haunted House.
People were watching and Angelina
looked very cross. Alice and William
wandered off, leaving her with Henry.

"Can I have a blue balloon now?" Henry asked Angelina shyly. "And can I go on the merry-go-round?"

Suddenly, Alice and William rushed up.

"You should have come with us, Angelina. We've just been on the swinging boat, and the helter skelter. It was fantastic!"

"It's just not fair," said Angelina crossly.

"You have to come on the Loop the
Loop rollercoaster with us. You just
HAVE to!" cried Alice.

"I don't like rollercoasters," said Henry.
Angelina sighed.

Suddenly, a clown walked by.
"Show starts in ten minutes!" he cried.
"Wicky wacky fun for all ages!"
Angelina smiled. "I bet you like clown
shows, don't you Henry?" she said.

At last she was free! She left Henry at the clown show and soon she, Alice and William were soaring up high on the rollercoaster. They loved it so much that they rode on it SEVEN TIMES!

Henry, meanwhile, wasn't having much fun at the clown show. As his eyes wandered he saw a big blue balloon float past. He just had to go and catch it!

A little while later, Angelina, Alice and William arrived at the clown's tent to collect Henry. But Henry wasn't there.

"Henry?" whispered Angelina. Her heart was in her mouth. "Where are you?"

The three friends ran through the crowds calling Henry's name. They looked everywhere. Alice even called up to the stilt walker because he'd be able to see across the whole fairground. But nobody had seen Henry.

At last they sat down on a bench. Alice tried to comfort Angelina and William offered her his hankie to blow her nose. "What am I going to do?" cried Angelina.

Suddenly, Angelina saw a blue balloon float past, with Henry running along behind, trying to catch it.
"Henry!" she cried. "Thank goodness!"

Angelina took Henry by the paw and
they set off through the crowds. Angelina
even used her precious coins to buy
Henry a big blue balloon.
"Look at the merry-go-round Angelina!"
cried Henry. "I love merry-go-rounds."

Angelina smiled as she helped Henry up
onto his favourite ride. "I love merry-go-
rounds, too."

Two Mice
in a Boat

It was bedtime but Angelina wasn't tired. She'd found her father's old Miller's Pond Boat Carnival trophy. "Oh Dad! I'm determined to win this year," she said.

"And how are you going to decorate
your boat, Angelina?" asked her father.
"Well," began Angelina. "It will be a
huge white swan, with gold thrones for
Alice and me, the Swan Princesses!"
"It sounds lovely dear, but don't count
on being teamed with Alice," warned
Mrs Mouseling gently.

The next day at school, Miss Chalk
announced the boat decorating teams.
"Priscilla with Penelope, Flora with
William, Angelina with Sammy . . ."
"Sammy!" said Angelina, shocked.
"Angelina!" spluttered Sammy.
"Alice with Henry," continued Miss
Chalk. Alice looked horrified.

"It's all about teamwork!" said Miss
Chalk over the din of unhappy mice.

Angelina and Sammy lined up to collect
their boat from Captain Miller.
"I wouldn't be seen dead in a sissy swan
boat," muttered Sammy.
"Well, you wouldn't catch me on some
stupid pirate ship!" spat Angelina.

"We're never going to agree," sighed
Angelina, looking at Sammy's plans.
"So we'll just have to try and . . .
"Work together," they both muttered.

The next day, they drew a line down the middle of the boat. They decided to decorate one half each. "Don't go over the line," warned Angelina sternly. "Don't worry, I won't!" said Sammy.

Just along the river, Alice and Henry were decorating their boat with sweets. "One for the boat, one for you!" they said in turn happily, popping sweets into each other's mouths.

On the day of the carnival, Angelina and
Sammy got ready early and went to try
out their boat on the river.
"It floats!" cried Angelina, when they
eventually managed to launch it.

The two mice turned round when they
heard a rumbling noise behind them. It
was the builder mouse, Mr Ratchett.

"Nice boat you've got there!" he said.
"What's she called?"
"The Swan Princess," said Angelina.
"The Pirate King," shouted Sammy.
"That's a big name for a small boat!"
chuckled Mr Ratchett as he carried
on up the road.

The mouselings jumped on board.
"I think we're sinking," said Sammy, as
he watched water seeping into the boat.
"I said that cannon was too heavy!"
cried Swan Princess Angelina, furiously.
"It's that stupid bird's head, more like,"
muttered Pirate Sammy.

They began to throw things out of the
boat as fast as they could, until there
was absolutely nothing left.

"We're floating now!" said Sammy. "Downstream!" shouted Angelina desperately. "Where are the oars?" "Over there!" cried Sammy, pointing to the oars floating between the cannon and the swan's head.

Meanwhile, Alice and Henry had nearly finished their boat, even though they'd spent quite a lot of time eating the decorations and felt a little sick!

Further upstream, Angelina and Sammy
were moving fast!
"We've got to stop!" yelled Angelina.
"I can see a tree stump up ahead!"
bellowed Sammy.
"We need some rope to loop over it.
Look!" Angelina had seen something.
"Vines!" They both said together.

As the little boat sped along, the two
frightened mice grabbed onto the vines.

"Puuuull!" screamed Sammy.
The vines broke away from the bank
and Angelina found the longest one.
They grabbed one end each just as the
boat reached the tree stump.

They struggled to loop it over the stump
and pulled themselves onto the bank.
"We have to get back to Miller's Pond!"
said a desperate and muddy Angelina.
They heard a chug chug behind them.
"Mr Ratchet!" they both said, relieved.

At Miller's Pond, the Carnival was
underway. Alice and Henry were
dressed as lollipops and their boat was
decorated entirely with sweet papers!

Suddenly there was a distant chugging
noise and everybody turned to look.
It was Swan Princess Angelina and Pirate
Sammy. They were floating along in the
sky, on the end of Mr Ratchet's crane!

Everyone at Miller's Pond clapped and
cheered as they were slowly lowered
towards the water.

SPLASH! They landed a bit too close
to Priscilla and Penelope Pinkpaws'
boat. It was decorated as a huge pink
ballet shoe. "Our lovely shoe!" they
squeaked. "Now it's soaking wet!"
Angelina and Sammy giggled together.

"The winners are Alice and Henry," said
Captain Miller a little later.
"But this year's prize for teamwork
goes to Angelina and Sammy!"

Mr Mouseling introduced Angelina to
his old boating partner – Sammy's dad!
"We never won a teamwork prize," said
Mr Watts. "We were always arguing."
"No we weren't!" replied Mr Mouseling.

Angelina and Sammy giggled.
"YOU keep the trophy," said Angelina.
"No, you keep it," replied Sammy.

The two mouselings, and their fathers,
carried on arguing and laughing until
the sun went down and it was time for
every tired mouse to go home to bed.

Angelina's Top Tips!

If Angelina is to become a
famous ballerina one day there are
some things she must remember to do . .

Walk elegantly

Sit prettily

Twirl energetically

Smile happily

Dance gracefully

Practise carefully

Angelina loves...

Pale pink tutus

Strawberry mousse with pink sprinkles

Raspberry milkshake with cream on top

Bright pink roses

Giggling with her best friends

And of course,

Dancing dreamily!

Do you love any of the same
things as Angelina?